D0572650

A HERO'S JOURNEY

ADAPTED BY DAPHNE PENDERGRASS
ILLUSTRATED BY DUSTIN D'ARNAULT, FREDERICK GARDNER, ALLEN TAM, AND ELISE HATHEWAY

Simon Spotlight

New York London Toronto Sydney New Delhi

SIMON SPOTLIGHT

An imprint of Simon & Schuster Children's Publishing Division
1230 Avenue of the Americas, New York, New York 10020

SIMON SPOTLIGHT and colophon are registered trademarks of Simon & Schuster, Inc.
For information about special discounts for bulk purchases, please contact
Simon & Schuster Special Sales at 1-866-506-1949 or business@simonandschuster.com.
Manufactured in the United States of America 0814 LAK
First Edition 2 4 6 8 10 9 7 5 3 1
ISBN 978-1-4814-2349-6
ISBN 978-1-4814-2350-2 (eBook)

56Ø1 4458 2/15

Manolo Sanchez came from a family of champion bullfighters. His father expected him to become a bullfighter too, but Manolo wanted to be a musician. He told only his best friends, Joaquin and Maria, of his secret dream.

Manolo knew he would have to find a way to be true to himself, but little did he and his friends know that they were not quite in control of their own destinies.

Two ancient gods, La Muerte and Xibalba, had placed a wager on which boy would win Maria's heart. La Muerte had faith that Manolo would marry Maria, but Xibalba wanted to make sure it was Joaquin who won her over. It was this wager that would change the course of Manolo's life forever. . . .

Soon after the ancient gods placed their bet, Maria's father, the general of their town of San Angel, decided to send Maria away to school. Before she boarded the train with her pet pig, Chuy, she gave Manolo a guitar with a special message on it: "Always play from the heart."

"When you come back, I will sing for you!" Manolo vowed.

Many years passed, and Manolo tried to live up to his father's expectation that he become a great bullfighter. His first bullfight was to take place on a very special day—the day that Maria would return to San Angel.

Instead of defeating the bull, Manolo put down his sword. "We don't have to hurt the bull!" he cried. Maria applauded Manolo, but the rest of the crowd booed and threw garbage at him.

Manolo's father was very disappointed. "You are no Sanchez," he said as he walked away.

That night General Posada threw a grand party to welcome Maria home. Manolo wasn't invited, so Joaquin, who had become a celebrated war hero, sat next to Maria.

Joaquin tried to be charming, but it didn't work on Maria. She soon left the table and headed upstairs to her room.

Meanwhile, Manolo wanted to see Maria more than anything. He stood below her balcony and played a romantic song on his guitar.

Maria was enchanted by Manolo's music. She hurried to meet him outside.

But when she arrived downstairs, she found Joaquin—with a ring in his hands! "Maria, will you marry me?" he asked. Maria was stunned!

Just then Manolo walked through the door. When he saw the ring, he and Joaquin started fighting over who loved Maria more.

"You two are acting like fools!" Maria yelled.

Before they could settle their argument, they heard a loud explosion from outside.

The town was being attacked by bandits!

"Tonight, San Angel is under my protection," Joaquin said, handing his cape and swords to Manolo. Joaquin fought bravely, and defeated every single bandit. Maria was impressed and grateful. She agreed to go on a walk with Joaquin.

Manolo was devastated. He was sure he had lost his chance at winning Maria's heart. Then his father and great-grandmother reminded him that Maria hadn't actually said yes to Joaquin's marriage proposal.

Manolo went back to Maria's house and asked her to meet him one last time.

The next morning Maria joined Manolo on a hillside overlooking San Angel. They watched the sun come up over the town.

"I will never, ever stop loving you," Manolo told Maria.

"And I will never stop loving the man who plays from the heart," Maria replied.

But just when they were about to kiss, a magical snake, sent by Xibalba to interfere and help him win the bet, slithered out of the tree. Maria pushed Manolo out of the way as the snake struck!

"No!" Manolo cried as Maria fell to the ground. He scooped her up and ran to find help. When he reached the town, Joaquin and General Posada were angry with Manolo for not protecting Maria.

Manolo returned sadly to the hillside to retrieve his guitar. "I will never see her again," he said. He believed that Maria had gone on to the Land of the Remembered, the vibrant and festive world where people go when they leave the Land of the Living.

"You want to see Maria again?" a voice asked. Manolo turned to see an old man standing in the shadows.

"With all my heart," Manolo said. Suddenly, the old man transformed into Xibalba. He snapped his fingers, and the world went dark.

When Manolo woke, he was in the Land of the Remembered. It was even more colorful and joyous than he had imagined! He was elated to be reunited with his mother, grandfather, and other relatives.

"I missed you so much," Manolo said to them. "But right now I need to find my love, Maria."

"We'll take you to La Muerte," said Manolo's mother, Carmen. "She rules the Land of the Remembered, and she'll know where Maria is." So, Manolo and his ancestors traveled to La Muerte's castle.

But they were in for a surprise. Xibalba was sitting on La Muerte's throne!

"The Land of the Remembered has a new ruler, all thanks to you, Manolo," said Xibalba. "La Muerte and I had a bet, and she lost. She bet that Maria would marry you, and I bet that Maria would marry Joaquin. And since you're not around anymore . . . who's left for Maria to marry?"

Xibalba then revealed that Maria had awoken and was safe in San Angel. It was Joaquin who had saved her. Manolo realized that Xibalba had tricked him into traveling to the Land of the Remembered.

Manolo was determined to get back to Maria. "Please help me find La Muerte," he begged his ancestors. "She can send me back to the Land of the Living."

The Sanchez family embarked on a dangerous journey to the Land of the Forgotten, where La Muerte was now the ruler.

They met the Candle Maker, an ancient god who was keeper of the *Book of Life*, which contained the story of every single person in the universe. The Candle Maker noticed that, remarkably, Manolo's pages were blank.

"You are writing your own story!" the Candle Maker said to Manolo.

He agreed to take Manolo to the Land of the Forgotten. "Yes, you must get back to San Angel," he said. "A bandit named Chakal is on his way to attack your town. I'll take you to La Muerte so she can send you back."

The Land of the Forgotten was a gloomy place, and the skeletons there were not vibrant and joyous, as they were in the Land of the Remembered. "Those are the forgotten," the Candle Maker told them. "Nobody remembers them, so they will soon fade away to nothing." If the town of San Angel fell to Chakal, Manolo and his family would also be forgotten.

When they reached La Muerte, Manolo explained to her how Xibalba had tricked him. La Muerte was furious! "Xibalbaaaaa!" she screamed.

Xibalba appeared, and he confessed that he had cheated to win their bet. But he wasn't about to let Manolo return to San Angel so easily—Manolo had to complete a task.

"You will have to face your greatest fear," Xibalba declared. "You must defeat every bull the Sanchez family ever finished in the ring."

Thousands of skeleton bulls poured into the ring. Manolo tried to deflect them one by one, but there were just too many. Soon the bulls crowded together, forming one giant bull. There was no way Manolo could defeat such a monster! He was going to lose!

But then Manolo picked up his guitar. Just as the bull charged toward him, Manolo began to sing.
The bull stopped and was soothed by Manolo's beautiful music. With peace in its heart and soul, the bull dissolved into petals that floated away on the wind. Manolo had chosen music over bullfighting, and in doing so he conquered his greatest fear: being himself.

Even Xibalba had to admit that Manolo had accomplished his task. A beam of light struck the young hero, and he was transported back to San Angel.

Manolo arrived in the town graveyard to find Maria and Joaquin facing Chakal and his bandit army. He pulled Maria in for a kiss before calling to Chakal, "Come and fight me!"

"You and what army?" responded Chakal.

To Manolo's surprise, the ancient gods allowed all of his ancestors to leave the Land of the Remembered, for this one day only. They appeared in San Angel and joined the struggle.

Manolo, Maria, and Joaquin rushed at Chakal, but he was fearsomely strong. After beating back Manolo and Joaquin, he grabbed Maria and headed for the bell tower.

Manolo ran to follow him, but the tower was collapsing as he climbed. Manolo's ancestors helped him to the top, and he was able to push Chakal away, freeing Maria!

"I'm done playing," Chakal said, preparing to attack again. But he was no match for Maria and Manolo.

The pair fought side by side, defeating Chakal and the remaining bandits together.

"There is one more thing we need to do, son," Maria's father said to Manolo.

All the people of San Angel and the Land of the Remembered crammed into the tiny chapel. Even Joaquin gave Maria and Manolo his blessing.

Everyone cheered as Manolo and Maria, the heroes of San Angel, became husband and wife.